Flying
Donald Crews
Greenwillow Books, New York

Greenwillow Books,
a division of William
Morrow & Company, Inc.,
1350 Avenue of the Americas
New York, N.Y. 10019.
Printed in Hong Kong
by South China
Printing Co.
First Edition
10 9 8 7 6 5 4 3

Library of Congress
Cataloging-in-Publication Data
Crews, Donald.
Flying.
Summary: An airplane
takes off, flies, and
lands after having passed
over cities, country areas,
mountains, and more.
1. Flight—Juvenile literature.
[1. Flight.   2. Airplanes]
I. Title.
TL547.C68 1986   629.13
85-27022
ISBN 0-688-04318-6
ISBN 0-688-04319-4 (lib. bdg.)

Gouache paints and an airbrush
were used for the full-color art.
The typeface is Helvetica Black
Italic.

For those
who make
my heart
soar.

Boarding.

Taxiing to the runway.

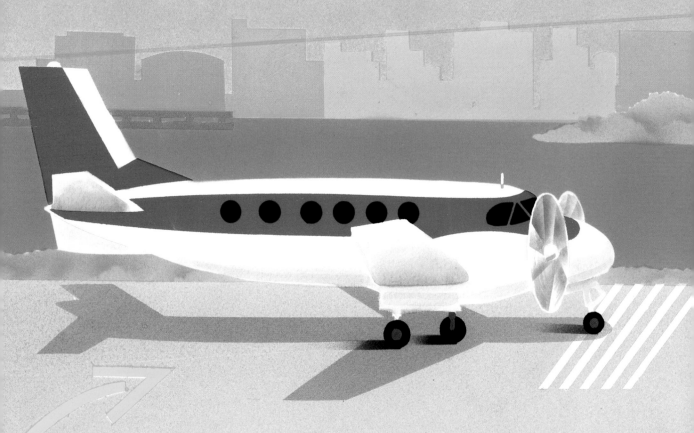

Ready.

Take off.

Flying over the airport.

Flying
over the
highways.

Flying over rivers.

Flying over cities.

Flying across the country.

Flying high over mountains.

Flying into the clouds.

Flying over the clouds.

**Time
to head
down.**

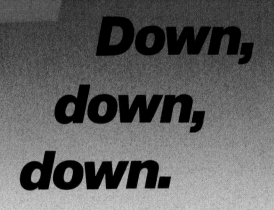

**Down,
down,
down.**

DOWN!

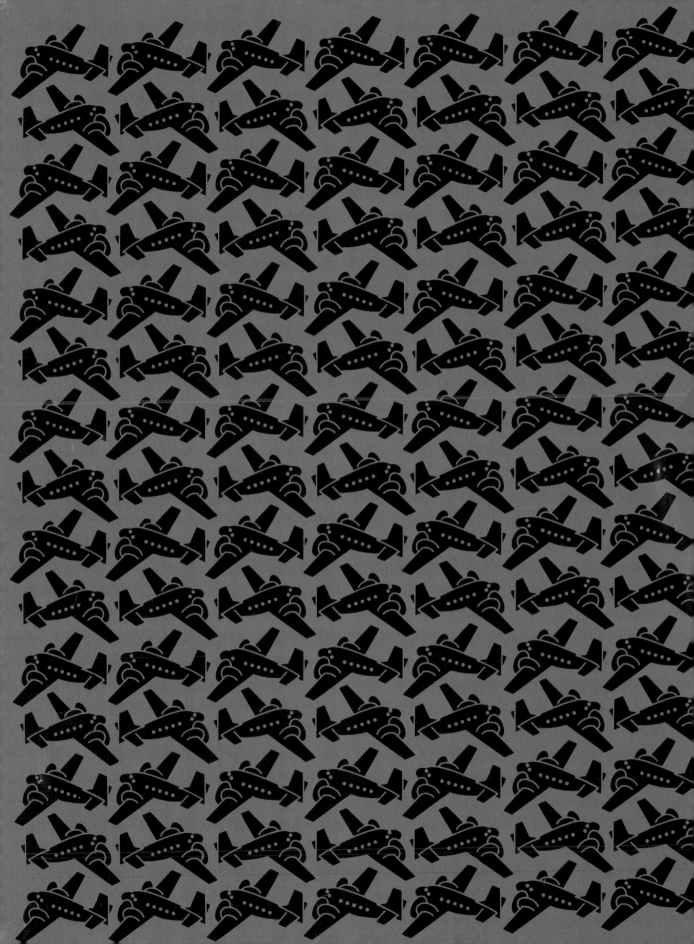

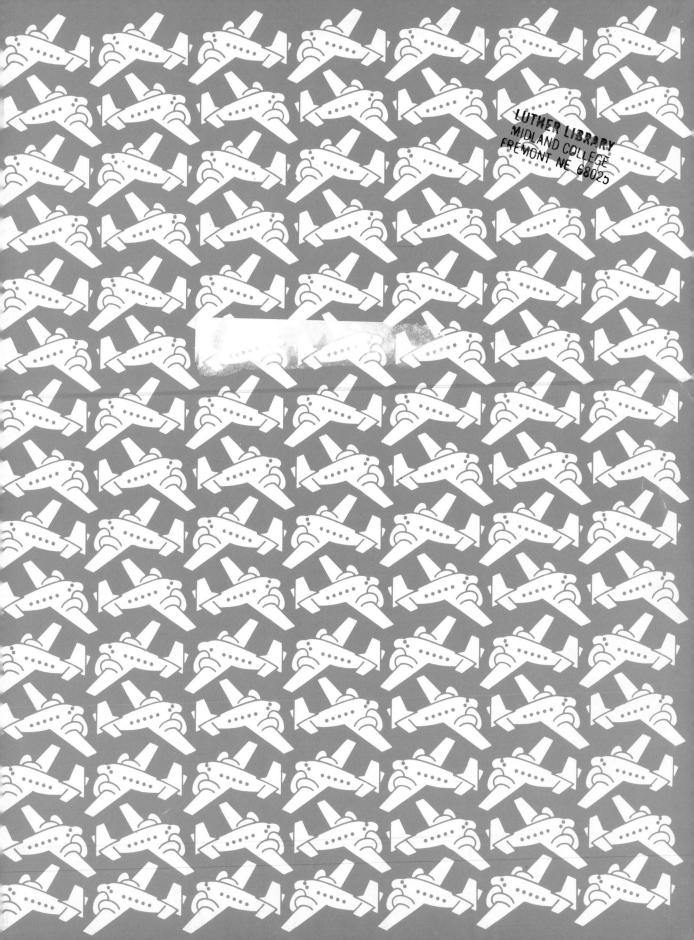